I0762337

CLOUDBREAKERS

Legend of the Sunlight Prince

Kenton J Moore

Cloudbreakers: Legend of the Sunlight Prince

Published in Canada by Soulforge Media

Cover Design and Interior Design by Kenton Moore

Edited by Victoria Helmink and Loretta Cameron

ISBN: 978-1-7770866-0-2

Printing in Soft Cover, Hard Cover, and E-Book by IngramSpark Publishing, USA.

As with every story I write, this work is dedicated to my children Lynaya and Korbyn. You are, and always will be, the audience my stories are meant for.

I would like also to recognize all my friends, family, and fans. Your tireless support is forever appreciated.

To my editors and proofreaders, thank you for being with me on this journey.

Legend of the Sunlight Prince
From the archives of the Imperial Libraries

I was a child when I first heard the tale of the Sunlight Prince. My mother had tucked me under my covers and sat on the edge of the bed as my father told the legend aloud in my room. I will never forget that night. It seemed as though the shadows in my room had come alive as the magic of my father's words echoed from the wooden halls. Light from the dancing candle flame drove the blackness away, and the forces of light and dark seemed at war, just as the forces of good and evil clashed as the story wore on. The wonder of myth had manifested in our home that night.

After becoming a historian for the Imperial Libraries, I made it my mission to collect information on this fable. Following years of laborious research, I have assembled, for the first time on page, the Legend of the Sunlight Prince. Here in this volume, told through the eyes of two children, is our Empire's most treasured tale. May it forever bring awe to our future children as it has for myself and those before me. Let it spread that most important of messages: There is always hope.

Aldous Corcoran
Headmaster Librarian
Imperial Libraries
Kingdom of Verdos

CHAPTER ONE

TAKEN!

A candle flame burned on a worn oak nightstand, casting its light across an otherwise dim room. A young woman stood in front of a tall mirror, pulling an ivory comb through her long light brown hair. Her hazel eyes rimmed with tears as her melancholy gaze fixed on something far beyond the mirror before her. She stood still while her hands continued their idle brushing; her satin night-gown hanging to her feet. Her trance shattered as she noticed the reflection of the door opening behind her.

"You are supposed to be in bed right now, Ben." She turned to face the timid brown-haired boy who crept into her room. His eyes sparkled with the same hazel colour as his sister, his face adorned with the same sharp jawline and narrow nose. Ben smiled at her and lowered his head. From behind his back, he produced a small box, brightly wrapped with purple paper and tied with a pink silk bow.

"I thought I might give you this. It is your birthday after all, and with Mom and Dad gone, you didn't get a party… so… well… here" he stammered and tossed the box on her bed. He flashed a coy grin and slipped out of the room. "Hope you like it!" he called out from the distance.

Lynn shook her head and smiled, her long hair swaying back and forth. She approached the bed and appraised her present before picking it up. Gingerly, she removed the wrapping and opened the box within. She gasped, and put her hand to her mouth. Inside the box was a beautiful necklace; a varied collection of coloured stones and wooden beads all strung together. Dominant in the piece was a pendant that resembled an ornately carved wooden L.

Lynn rushed through the door, her hair and gown flowing behind her. Outside her room, a staircase from the lower floor rose to meet a landing that connected three bedrooms. Lynn's room was the closest to the stairs, her parents in the center, and Ben's on the far side. Lynn hesitated, as she always did when she passed her parent's door, and for a moment imagined them coming out to surprise her. She sighed, knowing they wouldn't be there, and continued to Ben's room.

Ben was lying in bed when Lynn came through the door. A candle burned bright on the dresser opposite his bed. Her brother's hand-carved wooden practice sword stood against the far wall near the window. He pulled the blankets up, covering his face as Lynn walked in and sat on the foot of his bed. She smiled down at him, holding the necklace in her hands.

"Do you like it?" Ben whispered from beneath the covers.

Lynn nodded, and looked down at the necklace in her hands. She ran her fingers over the carved L. "I love it Ben. Did you make it yourself?"

It was Ben's turn to nod. He kept the blankets over most of his face, but the shine in his eyes told Lynn how proud he was.

"Where ever did you find the time to collect all these stones and carve these beads?" She asked, placing the necklace around her neck. "It must have been so hard to see them in the dark… and so dangerous too!"

"Calvin and I found them all in the woods and near the river. It took us a whole week to find them all! Plus we had to put some of them back because they were getting too heavy… but we only collected with adults around!" Ben trailed off a bit, but then sat up and continued his story. "Calvin's Dad helped me drill holes in the stones, and Mr. Merrihew at the tailor shop gave me the string to make the necklace, and I found the red-oak for the L and carved it myself! Just like my sword, only the L was harder to carve because it's so small…"

Lynn grinned as she ruffled her brother's hair. She leaned forward and hugged him tight. His small arms wrapped around his sister in response.

"Thank you, Ben. It's beautiful, and I love it as much as I love you. I'll never know where you learned to carve such wonderful things."

"It's easy. I just find a piece of wood that sings to me, sharpen my knife, and then I think of Mom. Or you. The rest just kind of… happens."

The mention of their mother brought a wave of grief. Lynn was about to open her mouth to speak when there was a large crash downstairs. Lynn leapt defensively from the bed.

"What was that Lynn?" Ben whimpered.

Lynn crept towards the door.

"I don't know. Stay here Ben. I'm going to go see."

Lynn peeked out of the door. Light from the candle burning in her own room spilled onto the landing, but the rest of the house below was too dark to see anything. Another crash came from the darkness below, like pots falling onto the kitchen floor. As Lynn stepped out from the doorway, something grabbed her arm. She almost screamed but managed to contain it when she realized it was Ben. He offered Lynn his wooden practice sword, held out in shaky hands.

Lynn made her way across the cold hardwood, gripping the carved sword tight in her fists. The light from Lynn's room felt a mile away, promising safety against the blackness. Below the landing, the house was so dark Lynn felt as though she was shuffling along the edge of a cliff. When at last Lynn arrived at her door, she was startled to find Ben had followed her. She shot her brother a withering glare for disobeying her, but kept any comments to herself for fear of scaring him further. Instead, she ducked inside her room and grabbed her candle and sconce from the nightstand. With their light now portable, they began making their way towards the top of the stairs. As they stepped down onto the first stair, a shape appeared at the bottom.

It was a Gargolye, a hideous winged creature known for raiding towns and hunting in the unending dark. Stories said they often kidnapped children. The beast stared at Lynn and Ben with glowing blue eyes. Long thin arms stretched out to the floor, with fingers tipped by sharp claws. Huge leathery wings folded against its back, and it walked on all fours. Lynn swallowed. Trembling, she eased Ben back toward her room with the flat edge of his sword.

Suddenly a young boy screamed from somewhere outside in the village. The Gargoyle turned its head to look in the direction of the sound. Lynn shoved her brother back toward her door.

"Run!" she screamed, waving the candle and sconce at the creature with her other hand. "Hide in my room! Hurry!"

Ben turned at her door with tears in his eyes. He looked past his sister at the Gargolye that was now crawling up the stairs on all four limbs like a lizard.

"What are you going to do?" Ben sobbed. Lynn looked at the Gargoyle and back at her brother. She backed away from the stairs onto the landing.

"Just hide, Ben! Hurry! Close the door and don't come out. I'll be okay!"

Ben slammed her door, leaving her outside with the approaching monster. It stopped halfway up the stairs and looked at the door, then back to Lynn. Lynn thought she saw a smile on its evil face as she lowered her candle sconce to the floor. As she stood back up, she took a fighting stance that her grandfather had shown her and gripped the sword firm with both hands. The creature sprung at her, sensing her intention to fight.

"You can't have my brother! I won't let you take him!"

Lynn put all the strength she could muster into a desperate down-stroke with the sword. She was lucky. The heavy wooden weapon contacted the monster on the top of its head. It fell to the floor at the top of the stairs unconscious. Lynn stood over her adversary, breathing heavy and trying to make some sense of what had just happened.

The silence exploded with the sound of shattering glass from inside her room mixed with a scream from Ben.

"Lynn! Help me!"

Before Lynn could get through the door, the sounds were gone. She fell to her knees just inside the empty room. Her window was smashed open and broken glass lay everywhere. Ben was gone. Lynn knelt motionless for a time, listening to the unbearable silence all around her. A groaning sound from the landing reminded her that there was still a Gargoyle in her house. She dove into her closet and hid on the floor under a pile of clothes, closing the closet door with her foot.

For what seemed like forever she hid there in the dark. The candle in the hallway eventually burned out, and what little light had made it into the closet was gone. Lynn cried to herself quietly in the darkness, sometimes sleeping, sometimes not. At one point she dared to whisper aloud into the night.

"Not Ben. Please Lord not my little brother. I promised to protect you. I promised…"

Lynn stroked the wooden L on her necklace until she fell asleep once more.

CHAPTER TWO
AFTERMATH

Sometime later Lynn woke, still under the pile of clothes. It was dark outside; a never ending night. She pushed her closet door open enough to see, and peered out into her room. The broken glass glinted in what little light the moon cast in through the bedroom window. Ben's wooden sword still lay by the door where she had dropped it. There was no sign of the Gargoyle anywhere. Outside the house, Lynn heard voices. Some of them yelled the names of their children, others called for help to search houses. As Lynn crept out of her hiding spot, she heard a familiar voice inside her own house. It was her grandfather, the town's baker.

"Lynn! Ben! Please, by the light answer me!" He called, a quiver in his voice.

Lynn tried to shout, but found her voice unwilling to muster more than a slight whisper. She was so tired, and still so very scared. She climbed to her feet and stumbled to the door, pausing to lean against the frame and gaze out warily. She almost expected to see the Gargoyle there waiting for her, but found crushing emptiness staring back. She stepped across the landing to the railing, and looked down into the living room. Her grandfather was standing in the center of the room, holding a torch and searching the wreckage in the kitchen. Mr. Merrihew was with him. Lynn tried to call out again, but still her voice refused to make a sound. As she tried once more, her grandfather turned and saw her.

"Lynn!" he shouted, and passed his torch to a startled Mr. Merrihew. Grandpa vaulted the stairs impossibly fast and scooped Lynn up in his arms. "Oh thank you! Thank the light you're okay!"

Lynn tried to tell her grandfather about the Gargoyles, and how they took Ben. Try as she might, no sound beyond a whimper would escape her. Her ordeal had nearly frozen her with fear. Gritting her teeth and fighting through the fear with all she had, Lynn managed a few short words.

"Monsters… Ben…" she whimpered, bursting into tears.

Grandpa held her tight in his arms and whispered reassurances in her ear.

"Hush now Lynn," he said, stroking her hair. "Hush now. You're safe. The shade monsters are gone."

Lynn cried against her grandfather's shoulder as he held her. It felt so safe in his arms. The sensation made her miss her parents though, and that thought made the tears flow freely.

For a long time, Grandpa comforted her. When Lynn finally stopped crying, he held her out at arm's length and looked in her eyes. Mr. Merrihew stood behind him, leaning against the railing and looking at the broken glass on the floor in her room.

"Lynn," Grandpa asked cautiously. "What is it you were saying about Ben? Where is he?"

Mr. Merrihew looked down at Lynn. She started crying again.

"It's okay Lynn, you're safe. Tell us what happened. The monsters are gone."

Lynn nodded and took a deep breath, forcing back her tears.

"The Gargoyles took him, Grandpa. I tried to save him, one was in the hallway. I told him to hide in my room and then I whacked the monster on the head with Ben's sword. I think I hurt it, because I knocked it flat out. That's when I heard Ben scream. When I got into the room..." Lynn choked and a few tears broke free of her eyes and ran down her cheeks. Grandpa took her up in his arms again. He held her tight, stroking her hair again.

"Oh Grandpa!" she sobbed into his chest. "There must have been another one in my room, and I sent him in there to hide alone! They took him because of me. He's gone now... because of me!"

Grandpa rocked her back and forth. Mr. Merrihew walked around Grandpa and put his hand on Lynn's back.

"Lynn..." Mr. Merrihew said, rubbing her back gently. "Lynn it's not your fault. The monsters did this... the Shade Wizard took your brother. It's not your fault. There's nothing you could have done better than you did already."

Grandpa shared a look of concern with Mr. Merrihew. The tailor saw a hint of tears in his friend's eyes; a deep sorrow that was brought about by losing sight of hope. Ben was his favourite little boy. The gentle old baker buried his face in Lynn's shoulder and they both cried together, wrapped in each others arms.

Mr. Merrihew turned away and walked into Lynn's room. He looked at the wooden practice sword Ben had made. It now lay on the floor just inside the door, a small stain of what looked to be blood on the dented tip of the blade. He looked at the broken glass, his torchlight reflecting in the shards like stars scattered on the carpet. Outside in the streets, the people of the town ran to and fro from house to house with torches. They called children's names in desperation. Ben was not the only child taken that night. Mr. Merrihew stood still as stone in the middle of the room, glaring out the window.

"Curse you, Shade Wizard. Curse you and your unending darkness."

CHAPTER THREE

LEGEND OF THE PRINCE

Lynn woke in a soft bed with thick covers and fluffy pillows. She lay still a moment, looking up at the ceiling and trying to figure out where she was. The last thing she remembered, she was crying in her grandfather's arms. She decided she must have passed out from exhaustion in the safety of his embrace and he had brought her to this bed.

Lynn looked around the room, waiting for her eyes to adjust to the darkness. A door in the room was slightly open, and light shone in through the crack. As her vision settled, Lynn saw plush carpets covering the floor, and paintings hanging from the wooden walls. There was a window to her left, and a fireplace to her right. Nothing but embers remained in the hearth, but she could still feel the warm heat driving away the chill that always lingered outside. A chair beside the fireplace held a set of clothes, neatly folded and waiting for her.

Lynn pushed the covers back and swung her feet off the bed. The fuzzy carpet was warm and soft under her feet. Lynn stopped about halfway to the chair. She had noticed angry voices outside the room. Cautious, she tip-toed toward the door as quiet as a cat, and was soon peering out through the crack. Right away, she knew where she was.

Lynn was in her grandfather's house across the street from her own home. As Lynn's eyes adjusted to the light outside, she saw Mayor Stoley staring out the kitchen window into the darkness, and Grandpa sitting at the table with Mrs. Stoley and Mr. Merrihew. They seemed to be arguing.

"There's not much we can do. You know that. Anyone able to fight has been gone for a long time now," Lynn's grandfather was saying, pounding his fist on the table. "The Wizard and his monsters are relentless, raiding more and more since this madness began. Every day those monsters take more and more children. Every day it is like the cold and dark become deeper. Light only knows what's happened to the adults who left for the forest. I lost both of my children, and now the first of my grandchildren as well! We have to do something before we have no children left, and we're the only ones who can because he won't take elders!"

Mrs. Stoley had her hands in the air, trying to calm Lynn's grandfather down.

"Now now, Mr. Mauris. We can't give up hope. We've all seen what that does to us. Besides," she hesitated. "The Prince may yet return."

Grandpa shook his head and sat back in his chair.

"No one has seen or heard from Arthur in years. For all we know, the Sunlight Prince could be dead. In the end, who's to say he could even stop this Shade Wizard? He's grown so powerful."

Lynn stood back from the door for a moment. "The Sunlight Prince?" she whispered. "Grandpa called him Arthur… I thought he was just a story."

"No," Grandpa continued angrily. "It's a silly wish to depend on the Prince. Even if he was alive and could help, no-one knows where to find him. Wisps are so rare now, and the

Guardians? They only care about themselves. We're on our own in the dark."

Mr. Merrihew leaned forward against the table. He knitted his fingers together as he spoke.

"I for one..." he began, looking from Grandpa to Mrs. Stoley and back again while he paused. "...would like to believe the Prince is alive somewhere, locked away in some dungeon where we could find him. However, I agree that it is a fool's hope to think he could save us. In the matter of our current situation, I believe that we should take more precautions to protect the children who remain. True as it may be that this is the first kidnapping in over a month, I think it's far past time for drastic action. We've lost contact with the other villages. The dark and the cold are getting worse, and food is scarce. We have to act now."

Mayor Stoley turned from the window to look at Mr. Merrihew. Lynn noticed that his eyes were red and puffy, like he had been crying for hours.

"And what do you propose we do, Mr. Merrihew?" Asked the Mayor, unfolding one arm to gesture towards the table. Mr. Merrihew lowered his head and rapped his knuckles on the table.

"I think we should hide the remaining children. Hide them somewhere safe where they can be protected. Somewhere like the mines."

The room fell silent. Everyone was looking at Mr. Merrihew, but he kept his head down and sat mute and still. A huge grandfather clock ticked away, the only sound in the house. After a time, Grandpa stood and walked away a few steps. He buried his face in his hands.

Lynn wanted to run and hug her grandfather. She wanted to tell him everything was going to be okay, and comfort him the way he had for her. She wanted to tell him the Sunlight Prince would beat the Shade Wizard and bring back the light, as well as all the missing children and their parents. She wanted so badly to console him, but she wasn't sure any of her words would matter. Grandpa himself had said that no-one knows where the Sunlight Prince is, or even if he was alive. Somehow though, Lynn knew he was. Something she had never felt before, deep inside her heart, whispered that hope remained. Her fingers rubbed the carved wooden L on the necklace Ben had made.

"What do we do about the children that have been taken? How can I so easily forget my daughter? Or Ben?" Lynn heard Grandpa say, his face still buried in his hands. Mrs. Stoley fought back tears, and the Mayor turned back to the window. Lynn saw the Mayor's shoulders begin to shake. Mr. Merrihew looked at them all in turn before he spoke.

"We can only pray that whatever the Wizard is doing with them, that it does not hurt."

Lynn backed away from the door. She heard Grandpa burst into tears along with Mrs. Stoley. Something hit the back of Lynn's legs and she found herself falling backwards onto the bed. She did not realize she had backed up so far from the door. Mr. Merrihew's words were ringing in her head. She could not believe what she had heard. They were giving up. They were going to do nothing, and all the while Ben and the others could be getting hurt. Lynn felt tears welling up in her own eyes. As she reached up to brush them away, her hand grazed the necklace again. She froze. The hope in her heart grew stronger.

Lynn ran her fingers idly over the carved wooden L pendant. A single tear ran down her cheek, but it was not sadness she felt. Something happened within her when she held the necklace. Her heart began to shout to her, its voice like a tidal wave crashing on the shore, carrying a power she never knew she had. She gripped the pendant tight in her fist as the storm raged inside her. A familiar voice whispered in her mind. A woman's voice, very similar to her mother's voice.

"You can find him, Lynn."

Quickly, Lynn scanned the room. She saw all the things she had seen before: the window, the fireplace with the embers still red, the chair with her clothes, a bedside table with an unlit lantern. Then Lynn spotted a closet hiding in the shadows between the window and the bed. She rushed over to it as quickly yet quietly as she could. Inside the double doors were lots of Grandpa's clothes suspended from hangers. There were jackets and pants, shirts, and shoes in the bottom. Lynn saw what she was hoping for tucked away in the bottom right corner of the closet: a leather travelers backpack.

Lynn scooped the pack out of the closet and threw it on the bed. She ran around to the other side of the room and quickly dressed in the clothes folded on the chair. The clothes held a soothing warmth within them from sitting so near to the fire. She threw her nightgown on the bed, grabbed the backpack, and crept to the window. The adults in the dining room were arguing again, but Lynn had heard enough. She knew that the adults were not going to help her. They would stop her if they caught her, and take her to the mine with the other children. Lynn slid the window open, the darkness and the cold immediately clawing at her face. She took one final gaze at the opened door, and then slipped out into the night.

The streets were dimly lit by tall post lanterns that always burned. The moon was up in the sky, clouded behind hazy dark shapes. The stars were invisible. The air was still and carried a biting chill. Inky black fog swarmed everywhere, threatening to extinguish all light. Lynn stalked across the street to her house, careful to stick to the deepest shadows and avoid the lantern light. Her front door had been locked, so she bolted around to the back and climbed up the lattice just below her broken window. Her room was dark as she climbed through the gaping hole where her window had been. Broken glass crunched under her boots as her feet met the floor. She searched in the darkness until she found some matches, and used them to light a fresh candle beside her bed

Scared that someone might see her light, Lynn rushed to gather the things she needed for her journey. She tossed the matches into the bag, along with a sleeping bag and some spare clothes and boots. Next she bounded down the stairs and got some bread, cheese, and dried meat from the pantry. As she ran back into her room, she nearly tripped on Ben's sword. She looked down at it for a moment, and then lifted it from the floor and lay it on the bed beside the backpack. When everything had been secured in the backpack, Lynn slipped a cloak over her shoulders and slung the pack. She barely felt the weight as she tied the waste belt. She stuck Ben's sword through her belt loop, and climbed back out the window.

A few feet from the house, Lynn turned back and gazed up at her window. The light from the candle she had lit cast a faint orange glow from within and out into the darkness. Lynn sighed and whispered to herself, stroking the pendant and feeling the rush of power once more.

"I promised Dad I'd always keep you safe, Ben. I'll find the Prince. I'll find you, and somehow we'll save you. Hang on, Ben. I'm coming."

With that, Lynn turned and disappeared into the forest. She never looked back again.

CHAPTER FOUR
IMPRISONED

Ben woke on a cold stone floor. He could hear water dripping, and a tapping sound like rats scurrying across the stone. There was a strong smell of mould and stale water. Wherever he was, it was not a nice place.

There was barely any light in the small stone room Ben found himself in when at last he mustered the courage to open his eyes. There was a bench that looked to be carved directly from the stone wall it ran along opposite from Ben, and a tiny window high above that let in moonlight and fresh air. The window had bars in it. Water stains ran down the wall, and small pools of foul liquid gathered in the corners before making its way in rivulets towards a drain in the center of the room. There was a single door into the room, made from heavy oak with metal bars all through it. As Ben sat up, he noticed he was not alone in the room.

A bunch of boys were scattered all around him. Some of them slept on the stone floor, some of them sat whimpering in the dark corners. All of them were filthy. A younger boy near Ben sobbed and looked up at him. He couldn't have been older than five. His eyes searched Ben's for any sign of hope.

"We aren't going to get out of here, are we? Will I ever see my family again?"

Ben shook a bit, but mustered his courage as he shuffled over to the young boy. He put his arm around him instinctively, feeling a need to protect the boy.

"Shhh now," Ben said, thinking of what his Grandpa or Lynn might say. "We'll be okay. You'll see."

An older boy sitting on the bench snickered and stared at Ben. Ben met the boy's glare, as a deep-seated emotion stirred within him.

"What do you know? The Wizard has us. His slaves come to take us away, and those kids never come back. You just got here, you've never seen it. Sometimes if it's quiet enough, you can hear them screaming."

Ben growled at the boy on the bench. His heart hammered in his chest, and a surge of rage lit inside him like a fire. He felt powerful, and he embraced it.

"You shut your mouth!" he snapped.

The boy slid off the bench and strolled over to Ben. He was at least a year or so older and much larger, but Ben stood his ground, holding the crying boy protectively in his arms. The boy from the bench said nothing. He cocked his fist back and without a word, punched Ben straight in the face. Ben took the blow without making a sound. The fire in his veins felt incredible. Gently, Ben released the young boy and stood to his full height. The boy from the bench drew his fist back to hit Ben again, but Ben was faster.

Ben had never felt anything like he did in that moment. His muscles felt like bottled lightning. Confidence overwhelmed him. He had made his practice sword himself by carving it from Red Oak, the hardest wood in all Hai'Leigh. He had made the necklace for his sister from the same wood. Clarity struck him when he thought of the necklace, and time seemed to almost stop for him. Before the boy from the bench even had a chance to blink, Ben's fist collided squarely with the tip of his nose.

Time fell back in on Ben as his aggressor collapsed to the stone floor. The boy's nose was bleeding, and he looked about to cry. Tears filled his eyes. Most of the other boys had woken up now, or were at least paying attention. They were all looking at Ben. He scanned around the room purposefully, his hands still clenched in fists. He wanted them all to know he would not tolerate attacks. As quick as it had come, the fire inside was gone, and Ben's hands went limp at his sides.

"I don't want anybody to say things like he was saying. My Grandpa says nothing good comes from being afraid. I know we're scared, but that doesn't mean we should make it worse by attacking each other."

A boy sitting against the wall near the door spoke up.

"Easy for you to say. You just got here. You will be afraid. When the slaves come again, and you see their eyes, you will be afraid."

"Maybe," replied Ben. "But courage is being afraid and still standing. I think."

Ben winked at the little boy still sitting beside him, but looking up at Ben with eyes wide in awe. Suddenly, the door clanked and opened up. Two big men came into the room. Ben froze in place, trying to show the courage he had just spoke about, but the guards didn't even look at him. They were giant men, with huge powerful muscles. The wore pants, but no shirts. Their wrists were covered with thick metal bracers, and they had rings in their noses and ears. Neither of them had hair on their heads, chests, or arms. They didn't even have eyebrows. When one of them turned to look in Ben's direction, moonlight briefly lit his face. Ben's blood froze solid in his veins. He immediately knew what the boy in the corner had meant. Where the man's eyes should have been, dark black holes into nothing stared back instead.

"Two more will come now," the man said in a voice that made the hair on Ben's neck stand. "The master has rested."

Emotionless, the two men stalked into the room. One of them stopped abruptly and turned back toward the door. He grabbed the boy who had spoken to Ben last, and threw him over his shoulder like a sack of flour. The boy kicked and screamed, but the slave's iron grip held him fast and he carried him out of the cell into the hallway.

The second big man stopped near Ben and looked down at him. Fear beyond anything Ben had ever felt washed over him as the empty pits in the man's face bore down on him. It was as though the void itself had replaced the man's eyes.

"If you're going to take me, go ahead and try!" Ben shouted. He realized that somehow the fire he had felt before had returned. Overwhelming fear and unbridled courage fought for control within him. His legs trembled, threatening to buckle. His fists clenched so hard that the blood drained from his fingers, turning his knuckles white.

"Not your turn yet," the huge man breathed. He leaned closer to Ben and drew in a deep breath through his nose, as though smelling Ben's very soul. "It will be soon."

The slave pushed Ben effortlessly against the wall and grabbed the boy from the bench with the bloodied nose. The boy didn't try to fight. He didn't even scream. Ben suddenly felt sorrow for punching him as the huge man lifted him onto his shoulder. For a moment, Ben thought he says the same empty darkness in the boys eyes, but before he could focus to be sure, the slave carried the boy out of the cell and slammed the door shut. Ben sank to the floor against the wall and hid his face in his hands, his body quaking from the tumultuous emotions he had felt. The little boy who had been crying crawled over and cuddled into Ben.

"My name is David," the boy said. "I'm five. Thank you for making me feel better."

Ben dropped his hands and looked down at David's face. Tears had drawn clean lined through the muck on David's young cheeks.

"My name is Ben. I'm ten, and I'm going to find a way to get us out of here. I just don't know how yet."

A boy curled up in the opposite corner of the room chuckled and leaned towards them, his shape spilling into the light like a ghost coming through a wall.

"If you need help with that, let me know."

Ben smiled when he recognized the voice and the face that came with it. It was his friend Marcus Stoley, the Mayor's son. Ben didn't say anything in response; he simply nodded to his friend and held David close in the dark.

CHAPTER FIVE
THE GUARDIANS

Lynn's eyes snapped open. Her campfire was burning an arm's length away. She couldn't see anything suspicious in her field of vision, but her instincts told her something or someone was staring at her. Gingerly, she reached out and grabbed Ben's sword from where it lay beside her backpack. When her fingers wrapped around the hilt, she started to sit up. As soon as she was completely upright, her breath caught in her throat.

Two bright yellow eyes shone out of the darkness on the other side of the campfire, seemingly floating in the night just above the licking flames. They were fixated, unblinking, on Lynn. Her heart raced. She gripped the hilt tight and brought the blade up in front of her face. The eyes came closer, and the creature they belonged to seemed to melt from the blackness.

A huge wolf stepped into the light of the fire. It was the biggest wolf Lynn had ever seen, standing almost as tall as a horse. The whorls of gray and black in its coat danced as it moved, making it look like a shadow coming to life. Most of its face was black except for a single white spot on its forehead in the shape of a diamond. Lynn shivered, unsure if it was fear or the cold. Or both. Despite the shaking, she sat in place with all the stubborn bravado she could muster. The sword tip quivered in the air before her as she found the courage to speak.

"If you plan to eat me, I have to tell you, I don't think I'll taste very good. Plus you're definitely going to get at least one bonk on the head."

What happened next made Lynn's eyes open wide with wonder. The wolf made a sound a lot like laughter and sat down on the other side of the fire. As he chuckled, ripples in his coat reflected firelight like a disturbance on a glassy moonlit pond. Suddenly something Grandpa had said came to mind, and stories from her childhood came rushing through her mind. She lowered the sword, confused but curious. She stared at the wolf in disbelief.

"Are you..." she breathed. "Are you a Guardian of the Forest?"

The wolf appraised Lynn for a short time. It was almost like it was staring through her, its eyes searching the depths of her own. At last, it lowered its head as if in a bow, and spoke in a deep growly voice that rumbled in Lynn's chest.

"I am indeed a Guardian, little one. And I have no doubt that if I were to eat you, you would not taste very good at all."

Lynn felt her fear wash away and she smiled childishly at the wolf. No one she knew had ever seen a Guardian, much less made conversation with one. They were creatures of myth; tales told by lost hunters who somehow found themselves guided out of the woods.

"What are you doing in the forest alone, little one? It smells as though you have not had a bath in days..." The wolf sniffed the air and shook its head in mock disgust. "You stink."

Lynn laughed out loud at the wolf, both because of its poor joke as well as its toothy grin. She never imagined in her wildest dreams that the legendary Guardians of the Forest would have a sense of humor.

"I do not stink!" Lynn said through fits of laughter, and then pleaded. "Do I?"

The wolf chuckled in his own deep laughter. Lynn felt comforted by the wolf. It was the best she had felt since before Ben was taken. Remembering her brother made the smile and the laughter fade, and Lynn looked down at Ben's sword. The wolf sat silently, waiting for her to speak.

"I'm in the forest because I have to save my brother," Lynn began. She told the wolf the whole story from the beginning. She talked about how her brother had made the necklace, and about the Gargoyle's attack. As she reached the part where she had overheard her Grandpa's conversation with the other adults, she paused.

"My Grandpa said Guardians only care about themselves. That we are all alone in the dark. Is that true?"

The wolf lowered its ears. Even with the unnatural depth of its voice, Lynn thought she could hear sadness.

"For most of the Guardians, yes. That is true. They do not trust humans."

"Why?" Lynn asked.

"Many reasons I will not burden you with, little one."

"Well," Lynn sighed and stared into the fire. "Grandpa thought maybe the Sunlight Prince could help, but I think he's just a story. I can help. I have to try for Ben's sake. So here I am. I came into the forest looking for the Ben, and for a long time I've walked in a straight line, hoping I would find him. I don't know if he's okay… or if he's hurt…. But somehow when I hold this necklace, I can feel him and I just know which way I have to go. One foot in front of the other, you know?"

Lynn fell silent. She was thinking about Ben, wishing he would suddenly leap from behind the wolf to surprise her. A tear rolled down her cheek.

"You are very brave, little one."

Lynn looked up at the wolf. He had leaned his head closer to her, nose down, almost looking up at her despite his size.

"To have come as far as you have," he continued, tilting his head to the darkness behind her, "all alone. It is an accomplishment not many can lay claim to. You must take heart, little one. If you seek your brother, or the Sunlight Prince, then friends have found you. We shall assist you on your journey."

"We?" Lynn asked just as the breath was stolen from her.

For the second time today, Lynn saw a sight that stunned her speechless. From behind the wolf's ears, a twinkling light appeared. Something small and impossibly bright rose into the night air; a ball of light flying on its own, like a star had come down to the earth. The star flew slowly around the fire, and stopped within arms reach of Lynn. Lynn gasped. The small ball of light had what looked like a tiny person at its core. Lynn knew instantly what she was looking at, but fought to believe it was real. Here, deep in the dark woods, was living proof of her favorite of Grandpa's stories. It was a Wisp.

Lynn was mesmerized by the little creature. This was something she had always dreamed about witnessing. Grandpa's stories about the Wisps played out in her mind. She remembered how he told her the Wisps helped the plants grow; that they were the living spirits of the forest. Without thought to her action, Lynn held out her hand, and the Wisp landed in her palm. As it settled onto her hand, the light faded, and Lynn was finally able to get a decent look at him in the firelight.

The Wisp was much bigger than Lynn had imagined them to be. He stretched to a height of about equal to the length of her forearm, but weighed barely anything. He had long blond hair and skin as green as spring grass. His features were surprisingly adult, except for pointed ears. He wore no clothing, but instead had strikingly beautiful markings tattooed all over his body. From his back grew four big transparent wings like those on a honey bee, and they seemed to sparkle, even in the darkness. He was the most beautiful thing Lynn had ever seen.

"My name is Surdy," said the Wisp in a surprisingly loud voice. Lynn realized his lips didn't move when he spoke. "What should I call you?"

Behind the fire, the giant wolf watched in silence. Lynn could barely speak.

"My name is Lynn…" she managed to whisper, still in awe over the Wisp in her hand.

"Are you speaking out loud? How do I hear you without your lips moving?"

Surdy laughed, this time with at least a smile on his lips.

"Wisps speak with our minds, Lynn."

"Wow…" she breathed.

Surdy waved his arm toward the wolf.

"The Guardian is known to us as Nightcoat. I suppose you could say that is his name. He was the very first Guardian of the Forest, and is the oldest and the wisest of them."

Lynn looked at Nightcoat and back to Surdy. She frowned then and looked at the fire, her backpack, and Ben's sword one after the other.

"Am I dreaming?" she whimpered.

Surdy giggled.

"Not at all," he replied. "Quite the opposite. You seem very wide awake."

"How did you and Nightcoat find me?"

"Aside from the fire?" Surdy danced in her palm. "We were traveling through the forest seeking other Wisps and Guardians. We saw that you were sleeping and could have carried on, but Nightcoat wanted to watch over you and make sure you were safe. Not many children come to the forest these days."

Lynn nodded. She looked up at the sky hoping to see stars or even the moon. There was nothing but darkness. Nightcoat followed her gaze.

"Grandpa says the forests are sick from the Evernight. He says when there was light in the sky, it was safe and beautiful in the trees. None of us have ever seen it… kids I mean. The adults talk about it often. But now…" her voice trailed off. "Now we never go near the woods."

Nightcoat lowered his head and lay down on the ground beside the fire. He breathed a deep sigh, almost growling as he did.

"It is true that the forest is sick. When the sun was stolen from the sky, the darkness began killing the trees and the plants. Eventually, there was no more grass. No more flowers. The trees lost their leaves and needles, and the forest became what it is today. The creatures of the forest are suffering. Many have died from hunger. For all this time, we Guardians have watched the decay of our home, and have not been able to do anything about it."

Lynn watched Nightcoat as he finished his story. She could see incredible pain in his golden eyes. Surdy flew into the air from Lynn's hand. The light engulfed him again, and he was once more a star come to earth.

"Is there any hope at all?" Lynn asked in a whisper, once more on the verge of tears. "Can the Shade Wizard be defeated?"

Surdy flickered and spun in the air. The light he shone grew brighter, and he floated closer to the ground. His light lit the bare dirt of the forest floor beneath him. Lynn watched with curiosity as Surdy began to dance in the air, his light getting brighter and brighter until he shone like a hundred candles. His voice in Lynn's head sounded strained.

"There is always hope, Lynn."

Lynn's heart hammered in her chest as she used her arm to shield her eyes from the bright light. From the dirt where Surdy's light shone, green grass started to grow. At first it happened slowly, but soon the whole spot of ground was a bright green like nothing Lynn had ever seen before. Lynn noticed two other plants growing in the center of the grass circle. They grew up high out of the ground on tall green stems. At their top, they formed disks of colorful petals. Lynn had never seen one in real life, but she knew of flowers from stories and pictures. These were daisies.

Nightcoat lifted his head and watched Surdy grow the grass and the daisies. When the petals finally reached as high as Surdy was flying, the light dimmed again, and Surdy settled down to rest on the flower as it swayed gently under his weight. By the firelight, the flower was the color of bright pink, like a fine silk. Lynn could not take her eyes off it.

"You see Lynn," Surdy began, sitting on his daisy flower chair. He looked older somehow, as if giving life took away his own. "The beauty of life is always right here in front of us, even if we don't notice it. Sometimes, it seems like the darkness will never end. Like everything will be black and hopeless forever, but that's not true. Sometimes it just takes a little light to see.

The darkness that the wizard brings is as powerful as it is because inside it, life loses all hope. Everyone forgets how to be happy, and instead they only know how to be sad. People believe that green grass and flowers don't exist anymore, but they do. They are just waiting for the light to return. They waiting for hope to return. That is why we need the Sunlight Prince. Arthur himself is also a powerful Wizard. The Wisps long ago gave him their power to save his life. His power alone could return light and hope, and defeat the Shade Wizard for good."

Lynn pondered this while staring at the flowers.

"Surdy," she asked. "Could the Sunlight Prince… Arthur… could he save my brother Ben?"

"We don't know for sure. But we believe he can."

Surdy grew bright again as he flitted over toward Nightcoat.

"How do we find him?" Lynn asked.

Nightcoat and Surdy looked at one another. Surdy flew around behind the wolf's ear and landed where he had been before revealing himself.

"The journey we are on is very dangerous, little one" said Nightcoat. There was no mistaking the grave tone in his voice. "It may not be safe for you to come with us."

Lynn's heart sank. She touched her necklace and felt the courage welling up inside herself. The woman's voice whispered, and Lynn couldn't be sure, but she thought Surdy had heard it too.

"Make them take you…" the voice said. "Make them see."

Steeling herself, Lynn stood. She was holding the necklace in one hand, Ben's sword in the other. She looked regal bathed in the firelight.

"I'm going to save Ben. If the Prince can help, I'll help you save him too. The world needs the light again. Just like Surdy said."

Nightcoat stared silent at Lynn as the fire crackled, and then his lips pursed into a toothy wolf grin.

"Hai'Leigh has always been protected by four towers known as the Temples of the Sun. They were built by the Prince many years ago. We think the Shade Wizard is using them to cast his darkness magic across the land. Surdy and I have checked three of them. Empty. We head now for the fourth and final tower."

Lynn nodded. "I know I should be scared… but I'm not."

"You have a strong heart little one," Nightcoat said in his growly voice. "Remember there is magic in love and hope. As long as you trust in it, it will guide you. Gather your things. You may climb on my back when you are ready."

Lynn started collecting her things. When she was done, she buried the fire with dirt, putting out its flame. Surdy lifted off Nightcoat's shoulder, lighting her way in the oppressive darkness. She paused before climbing on the wolf's back, looking down at the daisies in their oasis of grass. She bent and thoughtfully picked them, slipping them gently into her backpack. Then she grabbed Nightcoats fur and hoisted herself onto his back.

As Nightcoat darted off into the woods, Lynn thought about all the things she had learned tonight. She didn't understand all the talk about magic and love and hope, but she knew so far she had been following the voice that came to her when she held the necklace. Because of that alone, she had come across and befriended two creatures of legend deep in the woods. Nightcoat had broke into a run, so Lynn clutched his fur above his shoulders to hold on. She thought of the green grass and the flowers Surdy had made. She wished desperately that Ben could see her now, riding on the back of a Guardian with a Wisp. Ben would never believe her when she told him. She smiled to herself. For the first time in her life, she had seen green grass and flowers. The sight had done exactly as Surdy said it would. It gave her hope; and the voice in the necklace had led her to it all.

She wondered who the voice belonged to as Nightcoat shot deeper into the forest. She wondered if it really was her mother.

CHAPTER SIX
A THORN IN THE DARK

A robed figure strode down a torch-lit hallway, the flickering flames glinting off the deep purples and black in his cloak. His hood was drawn up, obscuring his face in shadow, and a sash hung around his neck and down over his shoulder into two flitting points. The sash was trimmed in blood red silk, and adorned with sharp symbols in the same red. Behind him, shadow and darkness ebbed like he was trailing black smoke from below his robes.

Purposeful and focused, he made his way to the end of the corridor and hooked to his right, descending down a spiral staircase made from stone. At the base of the stairs, he emerged into another hallway leading to a heavy wood and metal door where two huge muscled slaves stood guard. Their eyes were vacant and empty, two jet-black holes into nothing stared out where eyes should be. They did not react or greet the robed man as he marched between them and threw the door open.

Inside the jail cell, a woman with long flowing brown hair knelt in the muck. Her arms were lifted above her head, shackled by short chains to the wall behind her. She wore a white dress, long soiled by the filth of her captivity. A stone bench behind her offered her respite, but as if in an act of defiance, she chose to kneel on the floor. As the figure approached, she lifted her head. Bright green eyes shone up from a dirt encrusted face.

"You're late, Wizard" she spat. "Have you come to waste your time once more?"

The Wizard said nothing. He lifted a hand into the air and shadow spilled forth from his cloak. It wrapped around the woman's neck and chin, lifting her face until her body followed. When at last she stood on her feet before him, he lowered his hand and the shadow tendrils retreated beneath his cloak.

"Your words won't save you" the Wizard hissed, his voice almost as dark as his appearance. "I will wear you down in time."

Beneath the hood of his robe, an eerie blue glow began to illuminate his eyes and the features on his face. The smoke tendrils rose again, this time tinged at their tips with the same blue glow as his eyes. The tendrils rose slowly, wafting to and fro at their tips like the head of a snake about to strike its prey. They thickened and lifted higher and higher, creeping steadily towards the womans emerald eyes.

Even under the grime, there was beauty to the woman's features. Her chin and nose were narrow, cheekbones pronounced ever so slightly, and eyes almond shaped and piercing. Her jaw was set and sharp, connected to a strong neck that dipped into squared shoulders and a distinct collar bone. But under all the physical beauty was something else entirely that radiated from her. It was a powerful spirit. Unbroken. Unafraid. Hopeful.

The smoke tendrils suddenly darted into the womans eyes and she gasped. The glow burned where her eyes should be, as the darkness from the tendrils wrapped its way around her head, burying her from the neck up in writhing shadow. Sounds coming from her were muffled. The Wizard grunted in effort. The darkness deepened, threatening to swallow the entire room into the void. The very air seemed to thrum with power. And then it was over.

The smoke dissipated from the womans head and she slumped to the ground. The Wizard gasped for air, clearly fatigued. He knelt to the floor, placing a hand on his knees to steady himself. The glow in his eyes was gone, as was the shadow that streamed from his robe. Now, he simply looked like an old man in purple-black robes, kneeling in the dirt in a torch-lit cell. A sound began to echo in the chamber, and the Wizard wearily lifted his head.

The woman was laughing. Not a barrel laugh. Not the kind of laugh you would hear after a funny joke. But a weaker, proud laugh. A 'look what I have done' kind of laugh. Her head raised and she opened her eyes. Emerald green shone back at the Wizard.

"Again you fail."

The Wizard sighed audibly and stood, looking down at the woman.

"You vex me, child. I dislike puzzles and you are an enigma. Who are you?"

The woman shrugged.

"I'm no-one. Just a commoner from a simple town."

"You lie."

"Not at all," she laughed again, tilting her head to look up at her captor. "I have no need to lie, Wizard. Your magic is stolen. It won't work on me. That's why you will lose."

The Wizard turned his head to the sky.

"Why I will lose…" he repeated, almost as though he were testing the words. "You may think you know my story, but I assure you you are underestimating my power. I have stolen your sun. I have stolen life from your world. I have stolen your freedom. My minions steal your children, even now."

The Wizard knelt down again, moving close enough to the woman's face that she could feel his breath on her face. She held her ground and stared back.

"I will steal your hope. Even if it takes the rest of your short life."

"You will fail, Wizard. My Hope is not yours to take. It is out there," she nodded her head behind her, motioning to the world beyond her prison walls. "Coming for you. The dark will see a new dawn. Mark my words."

The Wizard laughed and stood again.

"The dawn…" he said as he strode to the door. As he pulled it open he stopped and turned his head to peer at her over his shoulder. The hood of his robe shrouding his face. "The dawn is in a cage of my making where it belongs. He will fall to darkness, as will you. Your clocks are ticking on, marching to an inevitable end."

As he pulled the door closed behind him, his final words echoed in the chamber.

"My clock has stopped."

The slam of the door marked the finality of his words, and the woman was once more left alone in solitude. Her eyes closed as she slumped to rest as much as the shackles would allow. A proud smile spread her lips.

CHAPTER SEVEN
GRANDPA'S FALL

Moonlight shone bright in a starless sky as Mayor Stoley and the other townsfolk guided the remaining children through the forest. Grandpa was not pleased with the decision to hide the children in the mines; however he felt lost and unable to argue any further. Lynn had vanished from under his nose. Both of his grandchildren were now gone, and without the Prince, there was simply no hope.

The children walked solemnly through the darkness, guided in silence by the protective adults. Grandpa watched as torchlight and moonlight danced on their faces. His mind wandered. He missed Ben and Lynn more than he could explain. Since their parents had disappeared, he had been responsible for their safety. When Lynn had decided to stay in her own home, Grandpa had not liked the idea, and had argued with Lynn every day for weeks. Eventually, he came to see the good in allowing them to be near what was left of their parents, so he had given his blessing. He loved them with all his heart, and now they were gone.

A tear rolled down his cheek, and he made no attempt to wipe it away. His whole life felt as if it was washing away from him. Sadness and despair clung to him like the darkness clung to the world. He plodded along the path one foot after the other, but he paid his footsteps no heed. As the group marched on, Grandpa turned his hollow eyes on the trees. He was dimly aware of the passing forms, but his gaze saw little more than the dark crevices of shadow between the lifeless husks of the forest.

For a moment, he saw the world as it once was under the beauty of the sun. He saw green grass and blooming flowers. He saw the trees, tall and full of life. He heard the sound of wind through the leaves. Woodland creatures dashed between the trunks of the trees, and birds flew in the sky. In a blinding flash, the reality of the world returned, and Grandpa plunged headlong into the sorrow of their kingdom.

The dust billowed up as his feet fell on the dry earth. No grass grew. No trees were green. No birds flew. Nothing bloomed. Their world was barren, lifeless, and black. The only sound the forest made now was the hollow echo of the people's footsteps.

Grandpa looked ahead and saw the gaping mouth of the mine. Against the blackness of the night, the mouth of the mine was somehow blacker still. A feeling of dread washed over Grandpa as his eyes fell on the void before him. It was as though his soul was being drained by the pit before him. Drowned by despair, he turned to head back toward the village. He felt like he was watching himself from miles away.

Mr. Stoley noticed Grandpa walking alone back toward the village. Quickly, he took a torch from his wife and jogged down the line of children being ushered into the mine.

"Where are you going?" Mr. Stoley called, but Grandpa did not answer. Instead, he continued plodding towards the village.

"We've reached the mine," Mr. Stoley pleaded, gesturing at the children filing into the shaft entrance. "The children will be safe here. Come on. There's nothing that can be done for Ben and Lynn. We have to focus on saving the children that remain!"

Mr. Stoley reached out and put his hand on Grandpa's shoulder. Grandpa stopped and turned around to face Mr. Stoley. The torchlight danced on Grandpa's face. Where Grandpa's eyes should have been, two dark black holes, blacker than the mouth of the mine, stared back instead.

"There is no hope. There will never again be light. There is only darkness now" Grandpa said.

Mr. Stoley's hand jerked back from Grandpa's shoulder. He swallowed before finding his voice.

"You are wrong Mr. Mauris," Mr. Stoley said, backing away from Grandpa. "That is the Wizard talking. There is still hope. There is always hope. You may have fallen Mr. Mauris, but I shall not. Go to the Wizard if you must, but tell him when you see him, that he shall never again take our children. There must be an end to this nightmare."

As Mr. Stoley turned and headed for the mine, he heard Grandpa's voice repeating into the darkness behind him.

"There is no hope. There will never again be light. There is only darkness now."

CHAPTER EIGHT
ESCAPE!

Ben pressed his back against the wall, feeling the cold stone through his clothes. His shirt was soaking wet, as it had been for days. He glanced at the streams of water trickling down the walls and decided it must be raining outside; the cell was far more damp than usual. If their plan worked, they might be able to see the rain. Ben and his cohorts waited silently for the slaves to come. The idea of escape had given them hope, and freedom was worth striving for. They had spent the entire day concocting their plans, and now it was about to come to fruition.

Ben heard the sound they had been waiting for, and gave the signal to prepare. Marcus hid against the wall on the opposite side of the door from Ben. David lay down in the middle of the room. At Ben's cue, he curled into a ball and started wailing. Ben looked at David crying on the floor and smiled to himself. The boy was a talented actor.

Outside their cell, Ben heard the footsteps of the approaching slave guards. His heart raced as a moment of doubt washed over him. He crouched against the wall, preparing to throw himself at the door as it opened. The doubt abated, replaced by conviction as he heard a key twisting in the lock. Ben drew a deep breath that lasted forever in that moment before explosive action. The door started to swing open, and as Ben had hoped, the slave guard poked his head into the room to look at the crying boy on the floor.

With all the strength Ben could summon, he threw himself against the door. The heavy wood hurt Ben's shoulder as he crashed into it, but at the same time, the door slammed shut on the guard's head. The guard collapsed to the ground unconscious. The second guard rushed into the room, throwing the door open just as Ben rolled out of the way unseen. With lightning speed, Ben sprung to his feet and dove to the ground directly in the path of the second guard. Before the guard had a chance to react, Marcus threw himself against the man's back like Ben had against the door. The guard toppled forward, tripping over Ben and landing face first on the stone floor. He did not get up.

Ben lifted his head slowly and looked around the room. Marcus was getting up from the floor, breathing heavily and wiping water from his brow. David was standing too, his eyes wide in disbelief. The cell was silent. None of the boys had believed the plan possible, but in the end had conceded to at least attempt it. Now here they were; two guards unconscious on the cell floor and the door hanging wide open.

"It worked" Ben whispered. The boys in the room that had refused to help crawled out of the shadows with eyes as big as dinner plates. They all looked at the guards on the ground, and at Ben. His plan had worked. He was their hero now. He had freed them.

"What do we do now, Ben?" One of the boys asked.

Ben quickly stuck his head out into the hallway. A torch burned on the wall farther down the stone hall. Ben could see two more cells on the same side of the hall as theirs, and solid rock on the other. The floor was also stone, but worn smooth from traffic over time. The roof had water and smoke stains, and the whole place smelled like burning pitch, dampness, mould, and body odor. Ben ducked back inside the cell and started to search the guards for keys.

"Well," Ben began. "I'm not exactly sure what we should do, but I have an idea. We try to get outside. Maybe we can hide in the trees from the monsters somehow."

The other boys nodded eagerly. After seeing what Ben and Marcus had just done, they would follow the pair of them anywhere they asked. Ben found a ring of keys on one of the guards and took it. He crept back to the door and peered out again. The hall was still clear.

"Okay," Ben said to the boys in the room. "Stay close. Marcus, watch the back okay?"

Marcus nodded, grinning. The other boys fell into line behind Ben. They were scared, but not one of them showed it. Ben stepped out into the hallway and led the boys towards the exit, keeping them close against the wall. When he reached the first door, he posted some of the boys as lookouts, and used the slave guards keys to open the door. The cell was exactly the same as their own, only it was empty. The group continued down the hallway and stopped at the next door.

The single torch providing light in the hall shone from a bracket across the hall from the door. Ben posted the boys in the same manner as before, and turned the key slowly in the lock. There was a soft click, and the hasp snapped open. Ben nudged the door open and poked his head in to get a better look. The sight that greeted him stole his breath.

The room was full of adults. They were all chained to the walls, and dressed the same as the slave guards. Ben motioned to the boys behind him to try and grab the torch off the wall.

When they finally got it free, they handed it to Ben, and he slid cautiously into the cell. Several boys followed him, curious to see what had intrigued Ben. They all gasped in unison when they saw the prisoners in the torchlight.

The men and women were all on their knees with their hands chained to the wall above them. They slumped forward, heads down, like they were all asleep. Ben walked along the line of them, a circle against the walls of the room. A drain in the center of the cell cast the amplified echo of drips as water fell down into it. Suddenly, Ben dropped the torch.

"Dad?" he whispered, inching towards a man chained to the wall. Ben reached out gingerly and touched the man's face. Ben recognized the face in the torchlight and started to cry.

"DAD!" Ben screamed and plunged into the man. He cried freely on his father's shoulder, his arms wrapped tight around the chained man's neck. The other boys in the cell backed away, uneasily looking from adult to adult.

When at last Ben pulled away from his father, his world shattered like a stained glass window dropped to the ground. Just like the slave guards, there were black holes where his father's eyes should have been.

"Ben..." his father whispered, his voice ghostly and distant. "There is no hope, Ben. No light will come. There is only darkness now."

Ben took a step back, shaking his head as tears stained his vision.

"No... Dad... it's not true. It can't be true. It can't be!"

The man that was once Ben's father stared back, not moving, barely even breathing. The abyss in his eye sockets fixated on Ben. He began to repeat what he had already said, as though he was trying to convince Ben to give up. One by one, the other adults in the cell joined in, repeating the same words.

"There is no hope. No light will come. There is only darkness now."

Ben fell to his knees as most of the other boys left the cell for the safety of the hallway. Despair flooded through Ben. He wanted so badly to run to his father and hug him again, but this man was no longer his father. Ben felt like everything in his world was crumbling around him like a house of cards.

As Ben succumbed to his sorrow, the slave guards that he and Marcus had knocked out began collecting the children in the hall. Their screams and protests echoed from the stone, mixing with the chanting of the adults in the cell. Ben did not care anymore if they took him. His father's words kept ringing in his head like a bell forged in the deepest pits of hopelessness. The empty blackness in his father's eyes threatened to swallow Ben into the void.

"There is no hope, Ben. No light will come. There is only darkness now."

Deep within his heart, Ben began to believe his father.

CHAPTER NINE
THE DRAGON'S CAVE

The moon was a soft and barely visible disk in the dark sky when Nightcoat finally slowed his run to a walk. Despite being on a serious mission, Lynn found that she was thoroughly enjoying the company of the Wisp and the wolf. Lynn had no concept of how long they had been traveling other than that they had stopped to sleep twice. At the last stop, there had been a hot spring where Lynn had been able to take a bath. Nightcoat and Surdy had jokingly voiced their thanks. They were both incredibly nice to Lynn, and told her all kinds of stories regarding sunlight and plants. Lynn felt her hope soar that one day she might see those things herself.

Nightcoat stopped suddenly, and Surdy flew off from his shoulders, disappearing into the trees. Lynn leaned forward and whispered in Nightcoat's ear.

"Where is Surdy going?"

The great wolf tilted his head and spoke to her in a whisper, keeping his gaze fixed on ahead.

"We have arrived at an entrance to a cave. It leads into the hidden valley where the fourth Temple of the Sun awaits. Surdy has gone ahead to make sure the way is safe."

Lynn reached behind her and pulled Ben's sword out of her pack. Nightcoat's ear twitched in her direction, and he turned his head back to speak to her.

"If there is anything in our way, that sword may not help you much. If it comforts you to wield it, keep it out, but you will likely have no use for it here."

Lynn nodded, but kept a good grip on the sword. It did somehow make her feel better just to hold it in her hand. She had come to realize over the course of their journey that somehow when she held the sword or her necklace, she could almost sense her brother. At times, it felt as though she could see him waiting in the dark. She focused on the woods ahead before something occurred to her, and she leaned forward again.

"Do you really think the Prince could be here? In the tower?" she asked.

Nightcoat said nothing.

"If he is… wouldn't that mean the Wizard could be too?" she continued.

Nightcoat sniffed the air, and then tilted his head to the side again to speak to Lynn.

"There are many types of magic in the land of Hai'Leigh. Some, like that which Surdy commands, can influence the world around us. Others are far more subtle, but still just as powerful. The items you carry have magic, and touching them guides you in small ways. You have felt it, haven't you?"

Lynn thought a moment and nodded. "When I hold the sword I feel brave, and sometimes I know where Ben is. The necklace guides me… and sometimes…"

Lynn's voice trailed off, and Nightcoat twitched his ears, patiently waiting for her to continue.

"Sometimes I hear a woman's voice in my head when I hold the necklace."

Nightcoat grinned and looked toward the cave again.

"There is a smaller type of Wisp known as a Nymph. They are the spirits of the forest, and often disguise themselves as leaves. In a time long ago, pilgrims use to seek the Nymphs out. Your distant ancestors. The Nymphs use to guide them on journeys, lighting the way to that which they needed most. The sword and necklace you carry are made from Red Oak; the most favored home tree of the Nymphs. Perhaps some of their power resides in the wood, and helps guide you to that which you desire most."

Lynn shifted forward on Nightcoat's back as she listened to his story.

"Where are the Nymphs now?" she asked.

"Wisps and Nymphs live in the trees and in the grass. They are part of the forest, and the forest is part of them. When the sun was taken, the trees and the grass and the flowers all started to die. So too did the Nymphs and the Wisps. There are very few left, Surdy being one of them. The Nymphs used their power to become leaves to search the Isle for the source of the dark sickness. They traveled on the wind throughout the forests, and eventually discovered the Shade Wizard's involvement. Before we could take action however, the Shade Wizard discovered the Nymphs and burned them in a great fire."

Lynn gasped.

"One of them managed to escape," Nightcoat continued. "She is the last Nymph left as far as we know. It was her who brought us the message, and Surdy and I have sought to gather the others and find Arthur ever since."

A tear rolled down Lynn's cheek. She hated the Shade Wizard. He was the cause of so much pain in Hai'Leigh. He stole the light away and made the forest sick. He hurt the Nymphs. He took Ben. Lynn's grip on the sword tightened, and she felt anger flood through her.

Suddenly, the whole forest erupted in red-hot light. A giant ball of fire soared into the night sky from the direction Surdy had gone. Nightcoat dropped himself to the ground.

"Get off me," he bellowed. "Quickly!"

Lynn jumped to the ground just as another ball of fire shot into the sky. Surdy flew through the trees towards them, stopping in front of Nightcoat. He was the brightest Lynn had ever seen him.

"Dragon!" Surdy barked, sounding out of breath. "There's a Dragon guarding the cave!"

Nightcoat looked off into the woods, back at Surdy, then up into the sky. The howl that came out of his mouth made Lynn cover her ears. The wolf took a huge deep breath and howled again. The ground shook and the trees swayed, blasted from their steady sleep by the force of the sound coming from Nightcoat. Nightcoat turned to look at Lynn, a fire in his eyes that made the hair on the back of her neck stand on end. She was no longer looking into the eyes of Nightcoat her friend. She was staring into the ferocity of Nightcoat the Guardian of the Forest.

"Count to thirty, then you and Surdy run for the cave. I will make the Dragon follow me so you can get inside safely. You must rescue the Prince!"

Before either of them could argue, Nightcoat vanished into the darkness. Moments later, another blast of fire shot into the sky. Nightcoat's howl shattered the woods again, and then there was silence. Lynn started counting out loud.

"One. Two. Three."

Surdy floated near Lynn, his light making shadows dance around the dying trees. There was no more fire, and no howls from Nightcoat.

"Twenty-eight. Twenty-nine. Thirty!" Lynn finished. She looked at Surdy.

"Can you fly just above my head? I can use your light to see when I'm running."

"Of course!" Surdy said, and then flew off to light the way.

Lynn and Surdy ran up a small hill, then down the other side. The trees were thick, and most of them burnt. The smell of fire hung thick in the air. Lynn was worried about Nightcoat, but at the same time felt herself hoping the Dragon had followed him, and wasn't waiting for them in the cave.

After running for what seemed like forever, Lynn found herself at the mouth of the cave. Surdy disappeared into it, and Lynn swiftly followed. The air inside was rancid, like rotting apples and mushrooms. It was huge, with roughly round walls rising to a hewn and jagged ceiling. Stalactites jutted from the roof, and stalagmites rose from the floor. Water ran down the walls and dripped from the ceiling, and glowing mushrooms grew in cracks and crevices all around. Lynn's gait slowed to a walk as she took in all the sights that Surdy's light touched.

Deep in the cave, Lynn and Surdy came to a fork in the path. To one side, Lynn could see a creek running off into the darkness, and she could hear rushing water from somewhere deeper into the blackness. The other tunnel was dry, and filled with glowing mushrooms. Surdy hovered impatiently near Lynn, waiting for the opinion of his guide. Lynn idly stroked the L on her necklace before making her way into the dry tunnel.

As they walked through the cave, Lynn stole a closer look at the glowing mushrooms. She noticed that it wasn't actually the mushrooms that were glowing, but small bugs that seemed to be eating the fungus. Surdy noticed Lynn inspecting the creatures, and hovered closer to explain.

"They're cave Nymphs," Surdy said. "The smallest type of Nymph or Wisp. They live in absolute darkness and feed on the mushrooms. Unlike us, they never stop glowing, and they can't speak at all."

"They're beautiful" Lynn whispered. "Still one constant light in the deepest darkness."

Lynn wiped a tear from her eye as they continued on. Surdy's light was better than any torch or candle Lynn had ever seen, and she had no problems with visibility in the depths. She started to wonder what sunlight would look like. The thought of seeing it in her lifetime made her hopeful. As they traveled deeper into the depths, Lynn noticed a small crevice in the cave wall to her right. When she stopped to investigate, she noticed that the crevice opened into a chamber of sorts beyond the wall.

The entrance to the chamber was little more than a crack in the wall. It looked like something had been digging at the rock for quite some time in an attempt to make the hole bigger. Despite her initial reluctance to enter the chamber, Lynn disappeared inside for a look. Surdy followed, and when his light lit the room, Lynn gasped.

Perched atop a rock pedestal in the center of the room was a huge egg. At first glance, it looked a lot like a huge chickens egg, only a little browner and about half Lynn's size. Lynn walked slowly around the circular room, staring at the egg. Surdy flew beside her for a while, and then hovered to the top of the egg itself.

"What do you think it is?" Lynn asked as she reached out to place her hand on the egg. The surface was cold, but not uncomfortably so. It was smoother than anything Lynn had ever felt before.

"It's a Dragon egg" Surdy said, his light dimming as he landed on the top of the egg.

Lynn looked up at the Wisp.

"Why is it here, stuck in this room? And why is it so cold?"

Surdy looked at the hole in the wall, then back at Lynn.

"If I had to guess, I'd say this is how the Wizard keeps the Dragon protecting this cave. Did you see the marks on the wall around the crevice outside?"

Lynn nodded.

"Yes. Scratches all over, like something had been trying to dig its way in."

Surdy flew up off the egg, his light brighter than it had been since they entered the cave. Lynn had to squint to see the Wisp.

"We have to get out of here, Lynn. If this egg belongs to that Dragon, he won't follow Nightcoat for long, and will come back to check on it."

Lynn ran her hand across the smooth surface of the egg. She felt a sudden sorrow wash over her. She found her thoughts drifting to her parents, and how they must feel being separated and kept from their children. Just then, Nightcoat appeared at the crack in the wall. Only part of his head was small enough to fit into the crevice.

"What are you two doing?" he growled. "The Dragon is coming back! We have to get away from that egg and into the valley!"

Surdy flashed towards the crack in the wall, but Lynn hesitated.

"Wait!" she suddenly called out. "Wait! I have an idea."

Lynn tried to lift the egg from the rock. She was surprised at how light it was, but found it awkward to carry because of its size.

"What are you doing?" barked Nightcoat. "If you drop that egg or damage it in any way, the Dragon will hunt us for all time!"

Lynn stumbled toward the crack in the wall. Twice she almost dropped the egg, but she stubbornly trudged on until at last she made it through the crack and out into the main corridor. Gingerly, she placed the egg onto the cave floor. As she stood up, she found herself face to face with the Dragon.

The eyes of the beast were blood red, and its skin was a silky black. Long white fangs stuck out of its closed mouth; chipped and worn horns hung from its head. Its huge leathery wings were folded down against its back and glistened in the dark like the surface of calm water. It was just as beautiful as it was terrifying. The snake-like head swung down to look at the egg and Lynn. Shaking, Lynn managed to find her voice. She was surprised at the confidence that came with it.

"The Shade Wizard took your egg so you would protect the cave that leads to the hidden valley, right? Why?"

The beast blinked, but otherwise made no motion at all. Lynn's fingers found the L on her necklace and gripped it tight. She felt the courageous fire ignite within her. Her shoulders squared without her noticing, and she stood tall and proud. A faint glow surrounded her body. The Dragon took notice, as did Surdy and Nightcoat.

"I have saved your egg, just as I intend to save the Sunlight Prince, my Brother, and all of Hai'Leigh. I believe the Wizard wants you here because the Prince is in the valley, and to guard your egg, you will not recognize friend from foe. Will you help us? Or will you eat us?"

Nightcoat and Surdy backed away from the Dragon, but Lynn stood her ground firmly planted behind the egg. She looked directly in the Dragon's eyes. She knew in her mind that she was scared, but for the second time since her brother was taken, her heart spoke with a different voice. A much stronger voice. The Dragon's head moved away, and it barked something that sounded a lot like a laugh. Short bursts of flame issued along with it.

"You are fascinating, little human-girl" the Dragon said, his head coming back down close to the egg. "It appears you have indeed saved my egg and for that, you have my thanks. I will not eat you. What are you called?"

Lynn bowed her head as Surdy and Nightcoat stepped forward again.

"My name is Lynn Mauris. These are my friends, Nightcoat and Surdy."

The Dragon's lips curled into a smile.

"It is a pleasure to meet you, Lynn Mauris. Your friends are known to me. I am called Calin."

Nightcoat sat on his haunches.

"Your method of greeting Guardians is questionable, old friend."

The Dragon's head shook from side to side.

"My apologies. These days it is so hard to know friend from foe. With so few Dragon's left, an egg is by far our most coveted treasures. It is rare enough for a Dragon to have one, but this has been the only egg since the Darkness came. Despite our initial hostilities, you three have done the Dragons a monumental service this day. You shall forever have my gratitude."

Lynn smiled. If only Ben could see her now, making friends with Wisps, Guardians, and Dragons.

"I am glad," Lynn quipped, bowing deep and mimicking the Dragon's formal speech, "that you will not be eating us today, sir."

Calin's laugh roared flames against the ceiling. A playful grin spread across his face as he cocked his head toward Lynn.

"I could not eat you even should I desire," he said, his lips curling back to reveal his huge teeth. "I suspect you would not taste very good. You stink."

Nightcoat and Surdy erupted in laughter while Lynn blushed.

"Why does everyone keep saying that? I *just* had a bath!"

The laughter subsided as Nightcoat and Surdy turned and began heading for the exit of the cave leading into the hidden valley. Calin gently bent and cradled the egg in his claws. He used the tips of his wings to help him walk toward the cave entrance while holding the egg. Once outside in the valley, Calin stretched out his wings but paused before taking to the sky. He looked down at Lynn and the others.

"Once I have ensured the egg is safe, I will return to assist you."

Lynn nodded and smiled at Calin. In a smooth motion, he pushed off with his back legs and beat his wings, soaring into the sky effortlessly.

"Another friend you have made today, Lynn Mauris!"

It wasn't long before Calin's black form vanished into the dark sky, but Lynn could still hear the beat of his massive wings. She turned to Surdy and Nightcoat her were both looking at her. Without another word, she climbed onto Nightcoat's back and the slipped off into the woods of the valley.

CHAPTER TEN
TO THE TEMPLE

The woman with the flowing brown hair sighed as she heard a key in the lock to her cell. She did not budge as the door opened, did not try to stand, and did not even look in the direction of whom she knew would be standing in the doorway. Instead, she grunted in disdain.

"When will you realize, Wizard? You cannot break me."

The Shade Wizard stood in the doorway in silence. There was something new about him. He had an air of nobility somehow that he never had before. He stepped into the room, walking right up to the woman and kneeling before her. Her eyes lifted to meet the darkness cast over his face by his hood.

"Some children here attempted an escape," the Wizard began, his voice cold with a touch of amusement. "They nearly succeeded."

The woman smirked.

"Your pride in defeating children says a lot about you, Wizard."

The Shade Wizard ignored the bait and continued.

"They were led by a boy of about ten years age. He was very brave. Resourceful. He was captured in your village."

The woman's breath caught in her throat as the Wizard continued.

"As I mentioned, he very nearly succeeded in leading the children out. Until he encountered one of my Hopeless in a nearby cell. That's where we found him, at the feet of a fallen slave, his spirit crushed."

"What have you done," the woman growled through gritted teeth. "Where is Ben?"

The Wizard smiled beneath his shroud, the corners of his lips barely visible in the dim light.

"On his way to the temple. He will undergo the change as all other fallen children have. He will become my hunter like all the rest. But that's not why I'm here."

The Wizard turned and walked to the door, motioning to someone outside.

"I've brought your new guard to meet you."

The woman wailed as she saw the man whom the Wizard ushered into the room. She felt what little hope she had left inside diminishing.

"I will leave you to your reunion," the Wizard said as he closed the door behind him, leaving her alone in the dark with the slave guard. "Enjoy your reunion Mr. and Mrs. Mauris."

In the dark, Mr. Mauris began his chant while his wife cried and screamed.

"There is no hope, my love. There will never again be light. There is only darkness now."

****

Ben was lost in despair. All he could hear in his mind was his father's words repeating over and over again like the drip of a leaking tap. He stared down through the darkness at the trees and land passing by far below. He could barely see them. He should have been elated to be flying through the air like a bird. Instead, he sagged in the gargoyle's arms as the scenery passed by. He had heard something from the slave guards about a temple, and the Wizard, but he was so deep in the darkness that he could not remember.

The gargoyle turned in the air, flopping Ben around like a fish caught by a hawk. A black starless sky filled his vision now. There were four boys along with Ben being taken to the Wizard at his Temple in the hidden valley. Four other boys who, like Ben, had lost all hope. Air rushed by and Ben felt a vague sense of speed as the gargoyles flew with the boys hanging in their claws. On and on they flew, silently and swiftly.

At one point the gargoyles banked so hard they nearly dropped the boys. They swooped down low just above the trees and shot along at an incredibly fast speed. Sometimes the tops of the trees whacked Ben in the legs as they flew past. Ben didn't even notice it. He didn't seem to feel pain at all, but was distantly aware of it. The rising sense of dread he felt deep within was silenced by a horrible roar of emptiness.

Suddenly, something in the forest caught Ben's eye. For the briefest of moments, he thought he saw a light like a candle flickering far below in the trees. His interest peaked for the span of a blink, but suddenly the void closed in on him again like the jaws of a great bear catching fish from a stream. He didn't care at all about what he saw, but something inside him motivated him to keep looking for the light, and so he stared with empty eyes at the dark forest. He never saw the twinkling light again.

****

Far below the trees, Lynn watched the silent shapes glide past in the sky. When they were far enough out of sight, Surdy emerged from under Nightcoat, his light shining a dim yellow in the darkness. Nightcoat breathed a sigh of relief and looked from the sky to Lynn and Surdy.

"That was far too close," the Guardian said nervously. "I think it might be a good idea for you to ride on my back with Lynn from now on Surdy. Your light can be spotted from a fair distance, even in the woods. We are close now, and we can not afford to be seen."

Surdy nodded and landed on Nightcoat's shoulder just in front of Lynn. His light dimmed and then winked out entirely, leaving the three with only the faint light of the covered moon. As Nightcoat took to running again, Lynn cast a gaze towards the sky. She had felt the voice rising inside her when they first saw the gargoyles coming toward them. It had not been courage this time that the voice spoke of, but rather a profound sadness. Sadness like she had never felt before.

With one hand holding tight to Nightcoat's fur, Lynn absently stroked the L on her necklace. She searched deep within herself to find strength she never knew she had and called it forth. She fought back the clawing despair that the voice in her head whispered into her heart. She pushed against it with all her resolve until at last it faded away. Somehow, she knew it was all up to her now. Her and her friends.

CHAPTER ELEVEN
RISE OF THE ORDER OF LIGHT

Lynn stared in awe at the Temple of the Sun. The huge walls and tall spires stood out against the night sky, seeming to glow even in the darkness. It was as if the Temple itself was fighting against the shadow, and refused to be dimmed by the lack of light. Nightcoat and Surdy seemed likewise awestruck by the glimmer emanating from the stone.

The Temple was square, with four towers at its corners. The walls were tall, and crenelated at their tops. A larger tower rose from the center of the square. Three rings of balconies ran around the central tower, with doors at each face. Lynn could see stone planters on the balconies that looked like they were once filled with beautiful flowers. She wished she could have seen the tower before the darkness came.

"It has been a long time since I saw this temple," Nightcoat whispered, turning his head to look at Lynn. "So much has changed since then. Let us hope the Prince is inside, and we can put an end to this darkness!"

Lynn nodded, and looked toward the gate that barred their way. The doors were massive and made of heavy wooden beams. In the center of the gate was a beautiful carving of a mountain with streams and meadows at its base. A giant shining star was rising behind the mountain. Lynn knew the star was the sun. She wished with all her heart that someday she would see it.

"How do we get inside?" Lynn asked, still gazing at the sun in the carving.

"This temple is a place of magic," Surdy began, slowly rising into the air. "Magic will open the door."

Surdy flew toward the carving of the sun on the gate. As he flew closer, his glow became brighter. His light fell across the door, and suddenly the sun in the carving began to glow. Soon, Surdy was lost in the brightness coming from the sun in the carving. The light that shone from the gate was blinding. It was like a million candles shining in the night. Lynn and Nightcoat both squinted, desperate to keep sight of their friend. There was a deep rumbling sound, and then the gate began to open.

Shielding her eyes with her arm, Lynn had to turn away from the gate. She was amazed to see that the light coming from Surdy and the carving was lighting up most of the forest around them. Green grass and flowers were appearing out of the ground, and the trees were turning green with leaves. It was just like when Surdy had shown her the flowers for the first time back at the campsite. Lynn couldn't help but smile. Life remained in the world, even buried under the darkness. The arm shielding her eyes dropped to her side and her eyes opened wide, taking in the sight before her.

As quickly as it had come, the light vanished. Lynn's heart sank. The night rushed back in darker that it had ever been before, and Lynn felt a wave of panic roll across her. She heard Nightcoat's voice from somewhere in the blackness.

"They know we're here! Surdy! Lynn! The gargoyles are coming!"

Lynn looked around frantically. She could not see a single thing. Somehow, when the light had gone away, the darkness that replaced it had blinded her almost entirely. She could hear the screams of the Gargoyles, and Surdy and Nightcoat calling to her, but she was lost in a dark world. Her hands shot out, desperately trying to grab hold of Nightcoat and climb onto his back. His voice sounded so far away. Lynn realized she was running.

Lynn skidded to a stop and stood still. She closed her eyes tight and tried to use her hearing like she did when she and Ben would play hide and seek. She could hear Gargoyles screaming and calling, and Surdy and Nightcoat yelling, but they sounded distant and almost as though underwater. Lynn opened her eyes. She found that some of her sight had returned, and she could make out shapes in the darkness. With a start, Lynn realized where she was. In her blind terror, she had run inside the Temple.

As Lynn's vision returned, she began to take in her surroundings. The floor was made of polished marble, and like the walls, it seemed to be glowing in the darkness. The room she was in was huge, and circled the base of the tall tower she had seen from outside. A series of marble pillars held up the roof, which itself was covered in a gorgeous painting of a sunlit forest. Lynn saw the Guardians in the painting, as well as Wisps and nymphs and other creatures Lynn had never heard of. At the bases of all the pillars were donut shaped planters that at one time must have held plants and flowers. Now, they were only filled with dirt.

In the center of the huge room was the base of the tower. On each of its four walls was an open door. Planters hung from the walls to each side of the doors. Inside the tower, Lynn could see a spiral staircase. She took a step towards the tower, but then stopped. It occurred to her that perhaps she should find her friends first. It was at that moment she noticed the sounds of fighting had stopped.

Lynn turned away from the tower to try and find the way she had come in. Two shapes appeared from the shadows and grabbed her arms. They were huge men with bulging muscles. Lynn froze in fear when she saw their faces. Instead of eyes, they had dark black holes, like the darkness itself was inside them. The two men lifted her right off her feet, and carried her toward the tower. Lynn tried to fight them, but it was no use. They were far too strong. She wanted to call out for Nightcoat and Surdy, but her voice wouldn't work. An intense fear swept over her.

The slaves carried Lynn through one of the doors and started to climb the spiral staircase. The inside of the tower was made from the same marble as the floors in the main room, and like the rest of the tower, seemed to glow in the darkness. Up the stairs they went, passing the first floor, and then the second. At the third floor, they left the staircase and stopped at another wooden door with the same carving as the gate outside. One of the men reached out and knocked three times on the door. There were muffled noises from the other side of the door, and then a click. The door opened inward, and Lynn gasped.

A tall man in dark purple and black robes stood in the doorway. The hood on his cloak was pulled up, shading his face in obscurity. Even though Lynn could not see under his hood, she knew he was looking right at her. He wore a crimson red sash, tapering to points at its end, that was covered in strange symbols. His hands were long and thin, with gnarled fingernails growing at the tips of his fingers. One hand held a tall wooden staff made from knotted wood. The top of the staff was a carving of a raven with its wings spread wide. But it was not his appearance that made Lynn shiver. From the bottom of his cloak, and up into the air behind him, tendrils and faint wisps of black inky darkness wafted through the air, like smoke made from shadow itself.

"The Shade Wizard" Lynn whispered to herself.

The Wizard reached his hand out and touched Lynn on the forehead. Lynn shivered, but stood her ground. She summoned the courage within herself, trying to emulate the inner fire she felt when she touched the necklace or Ben's sword. The slave guards arms held her tight, but her jaw was set in determination. The Wizard pulled his hand back as though he touched a hot plate.

"Child of the Thorn..." he murmured, the darkness behind him dancing ever so slightly as he stepped back.

The Wizard muttered something under his breath, and then drew himself up to a full height, looking down at Lynn. When he spoke aloud, Lynn was surprised to hear that his voice was rather pleasant. It had a smooth tone, and rang with confidence and authority. Lynn had expected much worse.

"There is much hope in this one. Where did you find her?"

One of the guards holding Lynn spoke. His voice was exactly what Lynn had imagined; deep, hoarse, and gravely.

"She was inside the Tower. A Guardian and a Wisp were with her outside. The Gargoyles fight them beyond the walls. A Dragon appears to be aiding them also."

Lynn smiled to herself. Calin had come to help after all.

The Wizard turned his head away. He reached up and pulled his hood back. Lynn's eyes opened wide. The Wizard had a head of long blond hair. It fell straight down, parted in the center, to lightly brush against his shoulders. Bright blue eyes shone from underneath thin eyebrows. Altogether, his features were very sharp and attractive. He was not at all what Lynn had pictured him to be.

"I suppose you have come for the Sunlight Prince," the Wizard said to Lynn. He was smiling, and Lynn found it quite unsettling. "Come. Let me take you to him."

The guards moved into the room, following the Wizard and dragging Lynn along with them. The room was much smaller than the one below, but still huge in comparison to anything Lynn had ever been in back home. Tables and desks were scattered all around, and each of them was littered with books and papers. Candles burned in holders on the walls, giving the room ample light for reading and writing. The Wizard led them around the staircase to the other side of the room. Lynn couldn't help but watch the shadow-smoke tendrils emanating from the bottom of the Wizard's cloak. They looked like ethereal octopus tentacles waving in the air as he walked. A circle of candles sat on the floor, and in the center of them was a group of young boys. Lynn's heart skipped a beat, and she tore away from the guard that was holding her with surprising speed and strength.

"BEN!" she shouted, dashing into the ring of candles and clutching her brother in her arms.

Tears flowed from Lynn's eyes. After all she had been through, she had finally found her brother. She hugged him tightly, and cried against his shoulder.

"Ben I was so worried! Are you okay? Did they hurt you?"

Ben was not answering. Lynn held him away at arm's length. The world ground to a painful halt. Where his eyes should have been, dark black holes stared back instead.

"There is no hope, Lynn. No light will come. There is only darkness now" he said.

Lynn's whole world came crashing down around her. Hope dissolved in a flash. The light, the flowers, the trees, Surdy, Nightcoat; everything she had seen and done vanished in a flood of sadness. Tears streamed down her face. This was not real. It could not be real. Distantly, Lynn heard the Wizard laugh.

"Finally! After all this searching. Here at last is the answer."

The Wizard strolled to the edge of the candle circle and knelt down. He reached out and placed his hand on Ben's head.

"You see young one? He has given up hope. The Darkness I have cast over this world eats away at ones resolve. It burns the mind. And then at last, when all hope has withered away to ash, the spell is finally let in. He is a Hopeless now. His will, his mind, his life force… it belongs to me."

Lynn barely heard the Wizard speaking. She stared into the black holes where Ben's eyes once were. One of the huge guards grabbed Lynn and pulled her out of the circle of candles. She stared at Ben, and he stared back at her with his dark eyes.

The Wizard stood and walked around the circle, where he grabbed a cloth that covered a huge square object in the corner of the room. He threw back the blanket, revealing a cage. Inside the cage was a man who almost looked as though he was the Wizard's double. The man sat on the floor of the cage with his knees up and his arms around them. Like the Wizard, he had long blond hair that brushed his shoulders and piercing blue eyes that shone even in the darkness.

"This girl and her friends have come to rescue you, Arthur," said the Wizard to the man in the cage. "Instead, they have brought your doom and the next phase of my spell."

Lynn looked from Ben to the man in the cage that the Wizard was talking to. The man did not make eye contact, he just stared at the ring of candles and the boys within it.

"How long," Arthur asked wearily. "How long must I be made to watch you spread your suffering, Helstor? Be done with it."

The Shade Wizard laughed. He walked around the ring of candles to a table and picked up a book and a vial of what looked like black sand.

"As long as it takes to break you, Arthur. I suspect, not much longer."

Lynn watched as the Shade Wizard threw a pinch of the black sand material into the air above the boys. It immediately turned to a dark storm cloud in the air, and the Wizard began to chant.

Tears flowed down Lynn's face. She stared into the hollow darkness where her brother's eyes once were, and he stared back at her. As the Wizard chanted his spell, Lynn reached up and her hands grasped the necklace. Ben's skin was starting to darken and become scaly. His arms and legs stretching out longer. Lynn thought of Ben carving the emblem. She thought of their love for one another, their life together, and the courage she had found that led her here. She became instantly aware also of Ben's sword. She could feel it, strapped to her back, as though it was pressed directly against her skin. No longer wanting to see her brother's transformation, she closed her eyes, searching to find the voice inside. Hoping it would tell her what to do.

The Shade Wizard threw his hand out toward the ring of candles. With his other hand, he slammed closed the book he had been reading. His chanting grew in volume, and the candle flames burned larger and brighter in response. The shadow tendrils from his cloak reached out and connected with the storm cloud the dust had made, pulsing into it, making it larger and darker. Wings began to sprout from Ben's back. Lynn's eyes were still closed. She had begun silently whispering as well. There was no voice inside her, but something was changing within Lynn. She was filling herself with her own voice, and it was louder and stronger than anything she had felt before. She saw Nightcoat and Surdy at the campfire. She heard their laughter. She saw Calin laughing. A bright glow began to emanate from within Lynn's fist as she gripped the necklace tighter. Ben began to blink.

Suddenly the Shade Wizard shouted. The candle flames shot so high that they almost touched the roof. A blinding light erupted in the center of the room from within the storm cloud above the boys. At the same time, there was a loud growl from behind Lynn, and the two guards that had been holding her suddenly fell to the ground.

In the sudden silence that followed, Lynn opened her eyes. She turned to see Nightcoat standing on the guards. They didn't try to fight him, his bared fangs so close to their faces. They looked confused, blinking up at the Guardian with hazel eyes. Lynn turned back to see everyone in the room on their feet and staring at her. Including Ben. He was staring right at her; with big brown unblinking eyes, looking exactly the same as he always did. In the cage Arthur was also standing, eyes wide in disbelief. The Shade Wizard stared at Lynn in absolute shock. His shadow tendrils were gone. A small star come to Earth floated into the room from a door leading out onto the balcony.

"You did it Lynn!" Surdy cheered. "You've saved your brother!"

Lynn was stunned. She did not know what she had done. All she remembered was truly letting herself go to the voice inside, but finding nothing, she filled herself with her own voice. Ben rushed out of the ring of candles and leapt into her arms. The other boys in the circle were looking around the room confused, and in fear of Nightcoat.

"You gave my hope back, Lynn! You came for me!"

Lynn sobbed and hugged her brother in return. She was so relieved that he was okay. She had no idea how she had done it, but Ben was back and that was all that mattered to her.

"This means nothing!" Helstor yelled. He threw his book aside, and thrust his hands out toward Arthur's cage. "If I can't break you, then I'll just crush you instead!"

As the Wizard started chanting once more, the bars of Arthur's cage started to shrink. Darkness flooded into the room again, and the tendrils from the Wizard's robe returned, wrapping themselves around the cage and choking it. Without a moments pause, Lynn drew Ben's sword from her back and handed it to her brother.

"Break the cage!" she hissed as Ben took the hilt in his hands.

As quick as lightning, Ben leapt across the ring of candles and darted into the cloud of darkness surrounding the cage. With both hands around the hilt, Ben hollered in effort and swung the sword in an overhead arc with all his might against the bars of the cage. As the wooden sword arced through the air, it seemed to pick up a glowing energy the closer it got to the bars. When at last the blade made contact, there was an earsplitting explosion, and the bars of the cage shattered in a hundred pieces.

"Nooooo!" Helstor screamed, falling to his knees. He looked drained and weary.

Light flooded the room, driving the darkness back. The tendrils belonging to the Wizard hissed and dissolved like steam into the air. Arthur was emitting light in the same way that Surdy did as he stepped forward from the shattered cage. He smiled down at Lynn and Ben, who couldn't help but smile back.

"I think you children have had enough of the dark by now," Arthur said as he made his way toward the cowering Helstor. "Let's fix that now, shall we?"

The Prince grabbed onto Helstor's collar and began dragging the pleading Wizard toward the balcony. Lynn and Ben walked after him. As they crossed out into the open air, the Prince looked down at them.

"Have you children ever seen the sun?"

Lynn and Ben shook their heads. The Prince nodded, and tossed the Shade Wizard to the deck before him. Helstor climbed to his knees before the Prince. Even in defeat, there was rage and malice in his eyes.

"You have no power to undo what I have wrought, Arthur. The life of the Kingdom is mine."

Arthur smiled at the kids.

"Nothing taken can ever match the power of what is given" he said, placing his hand on the Wizard's forehead. Arthur paused then and turned to the children.

"Shield your eyes, little ones."

Ben and Lynn held their arms up to cover their eyes as Arthur turned back to the Wizard and the horizon.

"It has been night for far too long," Arthur whispered as he held his free hand out toward the horizon. "It's about time for dawn."

Ben and Lynn watched, awestruck, holding each other's hands. Ben gripped his sword tightly, and Lynn still held on to the necklace. They both stared out at the dark horizon.

It happened slowly at first, a thin line of pink highlighting the tops of the mountains. Then the sky turned a shade of pinkish red. Clouds became white against the backdrop, and the moon began to fade. It was like the darkness was a blanket being pulled away from the whole world, coming down from the sky and washing into Helstor as he screamed wordlessly. Then the most beautiful thing Lynn had ever seen came over the horizon. It was a giant star. It was the sun. When the light fell across Lynn, she felt a tingling sensation in her skin and warmth like a fur blanket that had hung near a fire. The voice within her no longer whispered, spoke, or yelled. Now it sung.

"Sunlight returns" said the Prince.

Below them, the darkness seemed to peel back from everything. A wave of green washed over the forest. Leaves and grass and flowers sprung up out of nowhere as the sun touched the dying earth. In the planters on the balcony, gorgeous flowers grew up out of the soil. Fresh air mixed with smells the children had never experienced washed over everyone, and it was all they could do not to keep taking deep breaths. They had won the day. The world was alive again. Despair, sadness, darkness, death; it was all coming off the world and being drawn back inside the Shade Wizard as he shook under Arthur's hand. Ben and Lynn blinked at the Prince, trying to see through the light he was emitting.

At last Arthur dimmed and turned to the children. They blinked up at him, and for a moment barely recognized the man standing before him. As the light faded away to nothing, the children saw that Arthur had aged to a very old man. His skin was covered in wrinkles and laugh lines, and his hair was as white as the clouds in the sky. His eyes though, still shone with the same bright blue. He smiled down at Lynn and Ben standing side by side on the balcony. He reached out and touched the necklace around Lynn's neck.

"Where did you get this, little one?" he asked.

Lynn looked from the necklace to Ben and smiled.

"My brother Ben here. He made it for me" she replied.

"And the sword as well, I imagine?" asked the Prince.

Ben nodded. The Prince knelt down and put his hand on Ben's shoulder.

"You are rare children to have the use of magic" he began, looking from Ben and Lynn and back. "These items you make are powerful tools. Your sisters necklace binds the two of you, and your family. Your sword acts upon your intentions. Your love for one another, along with these items, allowed you to infiltrate and weaken Helstor's magic and save me; save the kingdom."

Arthur took Ben's sword and inspected it closer, a quizzical look on his face.

"You have somehow imbued these items with a powerful force. A necklace that can summon great courage and show that which is hidden to its bearer, and a sword that commands strength and fury when the time is needed. With time and training, you could both become great Wizards."

The kids looked at each other and laughed.

"We're not Wizards," Lynn said. "We're just kids."

Arthur smiled and handed the sword back to Ben.

"Kids you may be, but you have command of magic as well, to be able to use these tools. I imagine the act of touching these items brought you guidance and strength?"

Lynn nodded, but did not mention the voice that spoke inside when she had held the necklace or the sword. Arthur smiled.

"Magic is a very rare and very powerful thing," Arthur said. "I was given mine by the Wisps to save my life when I was but a child. Helstor..."

Arthur looked behind him for a moment before returning his gaze to the children.

"... Helstor stole his magic. From the Dragons, from the Wisps, from any magical creature he could. Including me. You two are the first humans I have ever seen to naturally have use of magic. It is indeed a new dawn."

Arthur stood and turned away from the children.

"What you have done today shall be remembered for a very long time. The two of you and your friends have saved Hai'Leigh. From this day forward, you shall be a Lord and Lady of our Kingdom."

Ben and Lynn beamed with pride as the Prince turned to look at the door into the tower, where Surdy and Nightcoat had just emerged. The wolf sat on his haunches, his tail wagging across the floor like a broom. Surdy sat atop the wolf's head. Arthur walked over and scratched Nightcoat behind the ears.

"It's good to see you, Nightcoat. You have done the Guardians proud this day."

Arthur nodded at Surdy.

"And you as well, Surdy! The Wisps will sing songs and praise your name."

"You have spent much of your power, Arthur..." Surdy said solemnly. Arthur shrugged and ran his hand through his white hair.

"Perhaps," he replied, turning his head to look at the children once more. "But I believe the kingdom will endure."

"What of the Wizard?" Nightcoat asked.

"See for yourself" Arthur said, stepping away and sweeping his hand to the side.

Helstor remained on his knees as he had been when the sun began to rise. His mouth was set in an open and wordless scream, his face grimacing in pain and anger. His whole body had become stone, a lifeless statue of the man he once was. His back faced the rising sun, and his hands were balled into fists at his side. Even the shadow-smoke tendrils had become stone, blowing away from the sunrise toward the tower.

"The sun was always there," Arthur explained. "Light and life, grass and flowers, they all carried on, but Helstor's spell hid it from all life. He plunged all living things into a darkness within their minds, and when they lost all hope, he fed on their life force to prolong his own and empower his own magic. When he tried to change the boys, Lynn was able to see inside his spell and take it apart from the inside. She showed me how to beat him, and when I was freed, I collapsed his spell in on itself. He will bother us no more. All who were transformed are returned to their original forms."

Arthur paused and looked at Nightcoat.

"We will need the help of the Guardians to return the children safely to their homes."

Nightcoat stood and lowered his head in a bow.

"The help of the Guardians you shall have," Nightcoat said. "Long live the Sunlight Prince!"

The others joined in the cheering, as did the children from inside and the two guards now freed from their curse. Down below in the courtyard, Calin and all the boys who had been Gargoyles before the sunrise cheered as well. The sound of all their unified chanting rolled out over the green forest.

"Long live the Sunlight Prince!"

CHAPTER TWELVE
REUNION

Grandpa was sitting on his porch tending to a pot full of flowers when Nightcoat came trotting up the road with Ben and Lynn on his back. Mister Mauris had not noticed them, and seemed to be lost in what he was doing. Lynn tapped Ben on the shoulder and pointed at him.

"I don't think he's seen us yet," Lynn said. "Should we surprise him?"

Ben smiled mischievously and nodded. The pair climbed down from Nightcoat's back, trying not to make much sound. Nightcoat sat on his haunches and watched as the children started sneaking towards the house. They stuck to walls and slipped behind bushed until they were at the edge of the porch. Lynn motioned for Ben to be quiet, and then crept to the base of his stairs.

Just as Lynn was about to leap out and surprise her Grandpa, she heard a woman's voice. Her heart hammered in her chest when she finally made the connection. The voice that had spoken to her each time she touched Ben's necklace now emanated from her Grandpa's porch.

"The flowers look beautiful Dad," the woman said. "I wish the children were here to see them."

Grampa smiled as he replied. "I have a feeling they'll see them soon enough. I want to be ready."

Lynn was frozen in shock. All the strength she had found through the necklace, all the power; it had been her Mother all along. That was what Ben had given her. That was the link Arthur had mentioned. The love of a whole family: a grandfather to children and grandchildren, a husband and wife to one another, parents to their children, and a brother and sister to each other; all imbued into a wooden amulet. He had given her all the rage and power of their love for each other. Lynn looked at Ben. His eyes were as wide as saucer plates. She wondered if he knew what he had done.

"Mom?" he whispered.

Lynn leapt around the corner onto the stairs, with Ben following close behind. There, standing behind Grandpa was their mother. She had long flowing brown hair, just like Lynn remembered, and beautiful shining emerald green eyes. Her eyes filled with tears when she saw the children, and her hands shot up to cover her mouth. Grandpa exploded to his feet.

"Lynn? Ben?" Grandpa shouted. He charged down the stairs and scooped the kids up in his big arms. Lynn and Ben's mother was close behind. As they laughed and hugged and cried, Ben noticed someone else coming through the doorway at a dead run.

"Dad!" Ben screamed, and raced up the stairs into his father's arms. "I saw you in the prison, Dad. You were under the Wizard's spell. I was so sad. I thought I'd never see you again!"

"You were there?" Ben's father cried, hugging his kids. "I heard your voices. Your Mom and I both did. You were calling to us, and suddenly we could see you! The spell was broken and there we were, your Mother and I, staring at each other in a prison cell!"

"We couldn't believe it," Mom said. "We knew you'd saved us. Somehow we could see you. We saw you save the Prince and we are SO proud you!"

Mom hugged Lynn tight, their tears running into one another's shoulders.

"You saved us. You and your brother. I'm so proud. I'm the luckiest mother in all Hai'Leigh!"

Grandpa wiped a tear from his eye and looked at Lynn.

"How did you do it?"

Lynn shrugged.

"It's a long story."

"Oh!" yelled Ben. "And Lynn and I are Wizards. The Sunlight Prince said so."

"Wizards!" Grandpa exclaimed. "Good gosh. That sounds like a story worth telling!"

As the whole family cried and hugged and laughed with one another, Nightcoat strolled away silently into the forest. In the sky, the sun shone bright.

www.ingramcontent.com/pod-product-compliance
Lightning Source LLC
Chambersburg PA
CBHW030612310726
48979CB00003B/678
9781777086602